You might have met
the Little Princess before!

The (Not So) Little Princess
COLOUR READER
What's My Name?

TONY ROSS
WENDY FINNEY

ANDERSEN PRESS

First published in 2014 by
Andersen Press Limited
20 Vauxhall Bridge Road
London SW1V 2SA
www.andersenpress.co.uk

1 3 5 7 9 10 8 6 4 2

British Library Cataloguing in Publication Data available.

ISBN: 978 1 849 39579 3

Printed and bound in Singapore by
Tien Wah Press

Contents

Chapter 1   1

Chapter 2   15

Chapter 3   25

Chapter 4   31

Chapter 5   39

Chapter 6   49

Chapter 1

The sun was a shiny yellow, the sky was vivid blue and the grass was greenest green – a lovely day had dawned over the castle.

The Little Princess was spending a quiet morning sitting in her comfy bedroom armchair busily trying to sew up a hole in her teddy's ear.

Poor Gilbert was getting rather old and thread-'bear'.

The Queen was happily making cucumber sandwiches for tea. She liked to help Cook from time to time.

But not everyone was having a lovely day. The King was pacing up and down the throne room,

scratching his head and frowning.
He had been doing this all morning.

Up and down. Up and down.
Backwards and forwards. Wearing
the carpet out and making his shoes
squeak.

Something was troubling him;
he was trying to find the answer to
a difficult question. Suddenly he
stopped in his tracks and said,
"I know what! I must call a meeting
of the most important people in the
land, they will know what to do."

And so he did. But he didn't tell
the Little Princess.

The Queen was the first to come
running in.

She was followed by the Maid, the Prime Minister, the Admiral, the General, Scruff the dog, the Little Prince, Puss the cat, the Doctor and the Gardener, plus two snails that were stuck to the Gardener's boots, and a duck who had just come in to see what all the fuss was about. "*Quack!*" it said, absent-mindedly.

There was a lot of noise as the royal household talked loudly amongst themselves, until the King raised his hand and declared, "I have asked you here today to help me answer a very important question . . ."

He paused, took a deep breath, then said, "The Little Princess has reached a certain age and a certain size, and she is not so little a princess anymore. We cannot keep calling her Little Princess when she is clearly *not* little and—"

"Stop waffling, dear!" said the Queen, beginning to fidget with boredom.

So the King coughed and tried again. "We have been calling our daughter 'Little Princess' for too long. We must call her by her proper name now and . . ."

The King was drowned out by a gasp of horror from everyone.

"But we can't do that, darling!" said the Queen, looking worried. "You do remember what her proper name is, don't you? We had to name her after the Old Duchess, and she had the most frightful name. An awful name . . . indeed an *ugly* name."

"That's very true, dear. I'd forgotten. Very ugly," muttered the King thoughtfully.

Meanwhile, the Not-so-Little Princess was still in her room. Suddenly, her tummy rumbled VERY loudly.

She decided to go to the castle kitchens to find Cook to ask for some royal nibbles. Mmmm! A toasted banana sandwich – that was her very best favourite.

But Cook wasn't there.

And the Maid wasn't in the living quarters.

And the dog wasn't in his basket.

And the Gardener wasn't in the garden.

Where was everybody?

Chapter 2

Back in the throne room, everyone was all in a tizzy about the Not-so-Little Princess's name.

"You should be the one to tell our daughter her real name. You are the King, after all," the Queen tried.

"Hmmm, I'm not at all sure about that," replied the King.

He was afraid what the Not-so-Little Princess might say if she knew how ugly her real name was!

"She is a bit scary sometimes!" the Queen sighed. "Do you remember the time when I was expecting little Prince Billy? She wanted him to be a 'her'. Oh, all the fuss she made about boys being smelly and not having the right toys! Goodness me!"

The King shook his head at the memory. "And when she wouldn't go to bed and we found her asleep in the dog basket!" he added.

"Oooh, and the time she wanted
two birthdays instead of one,"
butted in the Maid. She had seen
plenty of the Not-so-Little Princess's
tantrums. "So we ended up having
a birthday party nearly every day
of the year!"

"Oh, no!" everyone said together.

"It's certain," confirmed the Queen. "Our Princess just would not like her real name, and she would scream and scream and scream . . ."

All the royal staff shuddered in horror at the thought of the terrible noises the Princess was able to make whenever she was cross.

"But what can we do? We've still got to tell her her real name!" the King said in despair.

He didn't notice a small person tiptoeing in behind the throne. The Not-so-Little Princess looked around at all the people in the room. She'd arrived just in time to hear her father's words. The Princess was completely surprised. What was all this fuss about her "real name"? She had never thought she should be called anything other than "Your Royal Highness", "Your Majesty", or just plain "Little Princess".

She began to feel very cross.
"WHAT IS MY REAL NAME?!"
yelled the Princess in her bossiest,
loudest voice.

Everybody in the room turned to the Princess in shock. But nobody answered her.

"WHAT IS MY REAL NAME?!" she yelled even louder.

They gazed in silence at the Princess, whose face was beginning to go from red to purple.

Everybody looked nervously at each other. Then, all at once, they turned tail and ran off in different directions!

Chapter 3

The Not-so-Little Princess was
shocked. Why was everyone hiding?
Were they too scared to say her real
name? Was the name really horrid?

Her friends had normal names
like "Izzie" or "Billy". Sometimes
she had heard grown-ups calling
children odd things like, "You Little
Terror", and even, "Oi! Thingy!"

In the playground at school,
some of the kids called
each other names like:

"POO FACE"

"PIG NOSE"

"CABBAGE
FEATURES"

"BOG
BREATH"

"CLOTH EARS"

"SPOTTY CHOPS"

or, best of all, "SOGGY PANTS."

Once, in class, Harry Smith, who often shouted naughty things out loud, had called her "YOUR HIGHNESS LITTLE MISS HIGH AND MIGHTY VELVET KNICKERS". But the Not-so-Little Princess didn't mind people calling her names. She would just say the rhyme that went:

Sticks and stones will break my bones but names will never hurt me.

And she joined in laughing with
the rest of the class. It had made
everyone laugh so much that they
were told off by the teacher and
made to write lines as a punishment:

I must not Laugh in Class Unless
Teacher has Told a Joke
I must not Laugh in Class Unless
Teacher has Told a Joke
I must not Laugh in Class Unless
Teacher Has Told a Joke
I must not Laugh in Class Unless
Teacher has Told a joke.

She had also heard her
mum and dad call each other
"Sweetheart", "Darling" and
"Dearest love". All sorts of yucky,
soppy stuff.

Was her real name something
like that? Yuck! But she had to
know. So the Princess ran off to try
and find somebody who would tell
her this amazing secret.

Chapter 4

The castle was strangely quiet. No one was about.

The Princess headed to the laundry room in search of the Maid. At first glance it looked empty, but then the Princess spotted some legs waggling in the air from one of the laundry baskets. She knew those legs!

"MAIDY, WHAT IS MY REAL NAME?!"

"D-d-d-don't know," stuttered the Maid as the basket she had been hiding in tipped over. She tumbled out in a heap, a pair of pants sitting on her head.

Now caught, Maidy stood up, tidied herself and looked at the Princess. "You know, I never liked my real name," she said, trying to be sympathetic. "It's Buttercup."

The Princess shrieked with laughter.

"Well, my name's not THAT bad," said Maidy, annoyed now.

It's a terrible name. I hope mine is better than that! thought the Princess. And she couldn't stop herself saying, "Buttercup is the kind of name they give to a cow! You're lucky they didn't call you DANDYLION!"

And the Princess went on her way to find someone who could help her, leaving Maidy behind wishing she had been christened something else all those years ago.

As the Princess made her way through the castle, Prince Billy suddenly leaped out in front of her, his crown tilted so it fell over one eye.

"Oh, no!" said the Not-so-Little Princess. "What are you up to?"

Billy was beginning to turn into a cheeky little boy who played tricks on everyone and he loved winding up his big sister.

"You've got a silly name!
You've got a silly name!" he yelled in his babyish voice.

"Well, your name is even sillier!" she said.

"What do you mean?" he cried, running backwards. He knew that when his sister was in a mood like this, she was likely to give him one of her hard pokes with her best pointy finger.

"It's POOOOOOOOOOOO OOOOOOOOO!!!" she yelled at him, and chased him down the long hallway, pulling a horrible face and waving her arms like a monster.

"AAARRGGHH!" he squealed,
and he started to cry, before running
off to look for the Queen to tell tales
and get sympathy and sweets.

Everyone kept telling the
Princess she must try to be nicer
and set a good example, and for a
brief moment the Princess felt mean
for being horrid to her brother. But
this feeling soon passed. She didn't
have time to feel bad about it, she just
HAD to find out what her name was!

Chapter 5

The Princess decided to go outside
to look for the Admiral. She went
to his usual place, the pond, where
he liked to float in his boat. But he
wasn't there.

Then the Princess saw something
funny on the water. She looked closer.
There was a circle of bubbles floating

up to the surface! Squinting to get
a better look, the Princess could just
see the Admiral hiding under the
water, his face all scrunched up as
he tried to hold his breath.

But he couldn't hold it forever.
Suddenly, he burst through the
surface, coughing and spluttering.

He climbed out of the pond
looking embarrassed and stood
in front of the Princess. He was
dripping wet, but he didn't notice the
water lily resting on his shoulder or
the duck weed draped over his hat.

The Princess tried not to laugh.
She had to remember who she was
and try to be royal.

"What is my real name,
Admiral?" She looked at him
hopefully.

He took a deep bow.

"May it please you, your Highness – I don't know," he said. "What I DO know is that I also have problems with my real name. My parents called me Nelson, after the great sea lord. But I have never been able to live up to my grand name," he said sadly.

The Princess looked at him thoughtfully. Lord Nelson looked funny in the few pictures she had seen of him. "But didn't Nelson have only one eye? You have two! AND he only had one arm but you have TWO!"

The Admiral cheered up immediately. "And that is much better for swimming, of course!" With that, he jumped back into the pond and swam across to his little boat just to try out his two arms.

The Princess could see that the Admiral would not be much more use to her now, so she carried on her way.

She found the General hiding
in one of the sentry boxes, and he
also said he didn't know her name.
Although she was sure that she could
see him crossing his fingers behind
his back.

The Princess headed back into the castle. The Queen had always told her not to run because it was unladylike, so she ran-walked to find the next person to ask.

The Doctor was in her surgery, as usual, but she had her stethoscope in her ears and pretended she couldn't hear anything when the Princess spoke to her.

The Not-so-Little Princess even asked Gilbert, but he was no help.

By this time, she was beginning to think that everybody in the castle was telling rotten fibs, and that everyone except her knew what her real name was.

She decided to try one last
person, and ran outside again to ask
the Gardener. He was busy digging
up some leeks from the vegetable
patch, but, being an honest kind of
man, he said, "You must ask your
daddy. He will tell you."

Chapter 6

The Princess trudged back up to the throne room and found her father, the King of all the Land, hiding under the royal carpet. The Princess shook her head impatiently. As if she couldn't tell that the lump in the middle of the carpet was a person trying to hide!

She decided to ask anyway. "Please, Daddy, what's my real name?" the Princess said to the lump in the carpet in her sweetest voice.

The lump realised that it had been rumbled. Out came the King, dusting himself off.

He gave a deep sigh, took an even deeper breath and then said very quickly: "Princess Rubella Ovaltina Saliva Ignacia Eglantine the Third!" And then he scuttled away behind the throne for protection.

The Princess
was horrified.
"NOOOOOO
OOOOOOOO
OOOOOOOO
OOOOOOOO
OOOOOOOO
OO!!!!!!!!!!!!!!!!"
she yelled.

"NEVER! I
CAN'T BE
CALLED
THAT. IT'S
A TERRIBLE
NAME, AND
IT WILL TAKE
ALL DAY JUST
TO SAY IT!!!!!"

The Princess thought she might
burst into tears, and she could feel
her face going a deep crimson colour.

She began repeating the name
over and over, and it was even
worse than she had imagined:

"**R**ubella . . .

  Ovaltina . . .

  Saliva . . .

  Ignacia . . .

  Eglantine . . . the Third!"

But suddenly a great idea
flashed into her brain. Her face
changed from ANGRY...

... to HAPPY.

"Or ..." she said, feeling quite
excited at her own brilliance, "Or
...R.O.S.I.E. for short!" A beaming
smile now lit the Princess's face.

"Rosie! That is my name!
Those are the first letters of each
of my names put together – isn't it
wonderful?" she exclaimed.

And she grabbed hold of her
dad and swung him round and
round in a mad dance.

Then she skipped off down the castle corridor, past the shining suits of armour, past the Queen and Maidy and Cook, all the while trying out her new name to herself.

"Rosie . . . Princess Rosie . . .
Her Royal Highness Princess Rosie.
Her Mightiest Importantest Princess
Rosie. I like it. Yes, I like it. Everyone
must call me Rosie from now on."

The Queen smiled broadly. "If only we'd thought of this before! You are a Rosie for sure!"

Rosie beamed, and the entire castle breathed a sigh of relief and carried on about its business as usual. The sun went on shining down on all the land as if nothing had happened, because as far as it was concerned, NOTHING HAD!